The Gospel According to the Broken:

Poems from the Edge of Faith and Survival

Brandon Michaels

The Gospel According to the Broken:

Poems from the Edge of Faith and Survival

𝕏

@AuthorBMichaels

www.authorbrandonmichaels.com

Dedication

For the ones no one believed.
For the ones who were blamed,
shamed,
silenced,
and survived anyway.

For every soul who has slept in a shelter,
cried in a church pew,
bled in a bathroom,
or begged God for mercy and heard nothing back—
this book is for you.

You are not alone.
Your story matters.
Your scars are sacred.

Table of Contents

Part I: Poison in the Blood

The First Hit Felt Like God

I didn't mean to love it.
I meant to forget.
One hit,
just one,
and the lights inside me turned warm
for the first time in years.

It filled the hollow in my chest
so fast
I stopped asking if I deserved it.
I just needed it.

It wasn't euphoria.
It was silence.
No voices.
No guilt.
No shame screaming my name in the mirror.
Just quiet.

That first hit felt like God—
not the one in church,
but the one I begged in secret
to make it stop.
And this one?
This god answered.

It didn't ask for worship.
It just asked for everything.

So I gave it
my rent money,

my teeth,
my friends,
my daughter's birthday,
and the last picture of my mother.

It never said thank you.
But it always came back.

Spoon, Flame, Vein

The ritual was holy.
Spoon.
Flame.
Vein.

I didn't pray anymore.
Not with words.
I prayed with the click of a lighter
and the sting of a belt pulled tight.

The spoon held more salvation
than any preacher ever offered.
It burned clean.
It promised fast.
It didn't lie about the cost.

Vein didn't hesitate.
Vein took it in
like it had been waiting for this its whole life.

Sometimes I missed
and woke up hours later
on the floor,
half-dead,
piss-soaked,
with my face in the carpet
and no one calling my name.

Other times,
I floated.
Above the guilt,

above the noise,
above the body I stopped recognizing
in bathroom mirrors.

They say addicts don't believe in God.
But I did.
Mine was copper and flame
and an old bent needle I never threw out.

I didn't get high to feel good.
I got high to feel nothing.
And it worked
until it didn't.

Junkie Logic

I sold my phone
to a guy who'd screw his mother
for a half gram.
Told myself I'd buy it back tomorrow.
Never did.

That's junkie logic.
You make deals with yourself
you never intend to keep.
You lie so smooth
you forget it's a lie
until it's too late to care.

I stole from my sister.
Took the twenty from her purse
while she cried in the other room
because I promised I was clean.

I loved her.
Still do.
That's the part no one believes.

I gave a guy a blowjob once
for a fix.
Didn't think I'd ever say that out loud.
Didn't care afterward, either.
Not when the spike hit.
Not when the float came.

The logic was simple.
Get well,

then feel bad later—
if you even wake up.

I stopped feeling bad around year two.
Maybe three.
By then,
I had rules.
Don't use on Sundays.
Don't share needles.
Don't OD.
Guess how many I kept.

Cold Turkey Nightmares

They call it detox
like it's a cleanse.
Like it's spa shit.
Like sweating through your sheets
and puking in a bucket
is some kind of rebirth.

I didn't feel reborn.
I felt like I was dying
slow
with my skin inside out
and spiders crawling under it.

Every second stretched
like an apology I didn't believe in.
My legs kicked like they were trying
to run without me.
My teeth chattered like they knew
how many lies I'd told.

Day two,
I begged for death.
Day three,
I started hallucinating a woman I used to love
telling me it's okay
to quit trying.
That the needle missed me.

My sweat smelled like fear.
My sheets stuck to my body
like punishment.

Every blink was a new horror.
Every breath felt wrong.

They said I'd feel better after a week.
But by then,
I'd already crawled back
to the only god
that ever answered me
with silence.

The Dealer Asked My Name

The first time he asked,
I forgot.
Not because I was high,
but because I hadn't heard it
in days.

He didn't care.
Names were business.
He just needed something
to call me
when he handed over the bag.

It felt weird,
hearing it like that—
like a reminder
that I used to be someone.

He called me "bro" after that.
Sometimes "fam."
Never "junkie,"
though I knew
that's what I looked like
with my hollow face
and skin like wax.

One night, I told him.
Told him my name.
My real name.
And he just nodded
and passed me the rig.

That was the closest thing
to a friendship I had
for six months.

I cried once,
after he fronted me.
Not because I owed him.
But because someone trusted me.
Even if it was over a bag
I'd shoot into my neck
behind a liquor store.

He died last year.
Fentanyl.
I whispered his name
into a cracked spoon.

It felt holy.

Rehab Was Just a Room

They said I was lucky
to get a bed.
But it wasn't a bed.
It was a plastic mattress
with a sheet too thin
to cover the things I'd done.

There was no miracle.
No breakthrough moment.
Just four white walls
and a roommate who screamed at night
about things I couldn't unhear.

They took my shoelaces.
Gave me paper slippers.
Told me to talk about my feelings.
I said nothing.
Because the only thing I felt
was withdrawal
ripping through my spine
like wire and fire.

The counselor had soft hands
and eyes that looked past me.
He talked about steps.
About higher powers.
But I'd already been to hell
and I didn't trust stairs.

They called it healing.
I called it waiting.
Counting ceiling tiles.
Drinking bitter coffee
while my body screamed
for something stronger than hope.

I didn't get clean in that room.
I just learned how to fake it better.

Part II: The Bottle Never Breaks

Barstool Baptism

I found God again
at the bottom of a glass—
but this one didn't promise salvation,
just silence
and the slow burn of forgetting.

The bartender knew my name.
Knew I liked it neat,
no ice,
no bullshit,
no eye contact.

Every shot was a sermon.
Every swallow a confession.
Forgive me, Father,
for I've been drinking since noon.
Forgive me, Mother,
for not knowing when to stop.

The barstool held me better
than most lovers ever did.
It didn't flinch when I cursed.
Didn't leave when I cried.
Just spun
and rocked
and let me drown.

I was baptized in whiskey,
reborn in rum,
redeemed by the emptiness
of a liquor bottle I kept

like a trophy
on my nightstand.

They say alcohol is a poison.
But for a while,
it was a god
who answered
every time I asked
to disappear.

Whiskey and Wedding Rings

I said "I do"
with Jack on my breath
and a promise I meant
for about six months.

She wore white.
I wore hangover eyes
and a flask in my coat pocket
next to a pack of lies
I'd already told myself.

We danced.
We smiled.
We drank.
God, we drank.

I told her I'd quit
after the honeymoon.
Told her I'd quit
after the first kid.
Told her I'd quit
after I punched a hole in the wall
and she flinched
like a stranger was standing in my skin.

Whiskey and wedding rings
don't mix.
They scratch.
They rust.
They sink together

if you throw them hard enough
into the bottom of the same lie.

The last time I saw her,
she left my ring on the counter
and didn't even say goodbye.

Just silence,
and an empty fifth
on the floor
like the last guest
to leave the party
we never finished.

One Last Round

I said "one last round"
like it was a prayer.
Like it could undo the night
already crashing around me.

The bartender nodded,
didn't even blink.
He'd heard that line
from better liars than me.

It was always one more—
one more to calm the nerves,
one more to forget the fight,
one more to quiet the ghosts
scratching on the inside of my skull.

I drank until my lips felt numb
and the room started forgiving me.
Until my name stopped meaning anything
and my reflection looked like
someone who didn't owe anyone shit.

But the truth?
The truth always sobers you up,
eventually.

It's in the voicemail from your kid
you forgot to answer.
It's in the smell of vomit
on your own shirt.
It's in the dent in the hood

and the blood on the bumper
you don't remember earning.

"One last round"
is never the last.
It's the promise you make
to the bottle
right before it buries you.

DUI and D.O.A.

The lights in the rearview
flashed like a warning
from a life I kept running from.
I was drunk,
but I thought I could fake sober—
slurred charm,
chewed gum,
window halfway down
to let the guilt escape.

Didn't work.
They always know.
Cops can smell shame
even through cologne and excuses.

They said I ran the light.
I didn't even remember the street.
Said my eyes were glassy.
I said I was tired.
Said I failed the test.
I said nothing at all.

They cuffed me.
I laughed.
The kind of laugh
that tries not to cry.

It wasn't my first time.
Won't be my last,
if I'm being honest.

They booked me
like I was a number
in a system
I built with every drink.

Next cell over—
a kid, maybe twenty,
blood on his shoes,
couldn't stop shaking.
Said his buddy didn't make it.
D.O.A.
Drunk crash.
Head-on.

I stared at the wall
and pictured a coroner
spelling out my daughter's name.

Drunk on Father's Day

She made me a card
out of printer paper and crayons.
Said "You're my hero"
in shaky purple letters
like she hadn't seen me
passed out on the couch
for three days straight.

I cracked a beer
before I even thanked her.
Called it breakfast.
Called it tradition.
Called it nothing at all.

She sat next to me
in silence.
Watched cartoons
while I drowned in static.
I don't remember what we watched.
Just the sound of her straw
scraping the bottom of a juice box
while I opened my third tallboy.

Later,
I yelled at her for something—
I can't even remember what.
She flinched
like she'd seen this movie before.
Spoiler:
It doesn't end well.

When she went to her room,
I cried in the kitchen
with the water running
so she wouldn't hear
how empty I'd become.

She still gave me that card.
Still smiled.
Still called me "Dad"
like it meant something.
And I—
I drank
until I forgot how to deserve her.

Thirst Like a Curse

It wasn't just a drink.
It was a need.
A voice in my throat
that never shut up.
A pulse in my jaw
that beat louder than reason.

Thirst,
not like water,
but like fire—
a dry, angry burn
that nothing could quiet
except the bottle.

It followed me everywhere.
To church.
To court.
To the hospital room
where my mother lay dying
while I smelled like gin
and called it grief.

I tried to quit
like I tried to pray—
desperate,
empty,
and halfway lying to myself.

My hands shook
like they missed the bottle

more than they missed her.
My tongue felt foreign
without poison on it.
Everything tasted like guilt
when I was sober.

They say it's a disease.
But it felt more like a curse.
Something passed down in blood
or anger
or silence at the dinner table.

I drank to quiet it.
To kill it.
But it always came back,
thirsty.

Part III: Sold Bodies, Stolen Names

Motel Mirrors Lie

The mirror in that room
told me I was still pretty.
But motel mirrors lie.
They soften bruises.
They blur track marks.
They never tell you
how empty your eyes look
when you stop pretending
you're doing this by choice.

Room 112.
Flickering light.
Bedspread older than my last name.
He asked if I was clean.
I said yes.
He didn't ask what I meant.

I stared at the mirror
while he climbed on top.
Tried to imagine
I was somewhere else.
Someone else.
Someone who didn't measure her worth
in twenty-dollar bills
and silence.

After he left,
I washed my skin
like it was the problem.
Counted the money

like it mattered.
Tried to see myself
in that mirror again—
but it was too fogged up
with lies and breath
to show anything real.

So I stopped looking.
I just turned off the light.

Paid for Silence

He didn't want the talking kind.
Said "No stories. No names. Just do it."
I nodded.
Because silence pays more.

It's easier
when you shut off the part of yourself
that still wants to be held
without a price tag.

He smelled like cigarettes and mouthwash.
Like shame scrubbed with effort.
His eyes never met mine—
just flickered
like he was afraid
I'd remind him I was human.

I bit the inside of my cheek
to keep from screaming.
Not in pain.
Not even in fear.
Just to stop the truth
from spilling out.

I used to sing
in the church choir.
Used to write poems
about falling in love.
Now I count cash in a sock drawer
and memorize license plates

in case they don't pay
or forget who I am
beneath the fake name
and broken mascara.

He left fifty on the dresser.
More than I asked for.
As if money
could make me forget
that I'd once had a voice.

Craigslist Resurrection

I posted the ad
under "Casual Encounters."
Said I was 23.
Said I was clean.
Said nothing true
except the price.

He replied with two words:
"You up?"
I was.
Barely.

Met him at a motel
where the curtains never opened
and the Bible had water damage.
He didn't ask why I did it.
Didn't care that I shook
when he touched me
like he was waking a corpse.

Craigslist made it feel distant.
Just words.
Just screen names.
Just me pretending I was still in control.

But that night,
when it was over,
I stared at the bathroom tile
and thought:
"Maybe I'm not dead yet."

Because dead people don't feel shame.
And I still felt all of it.
Burning under my skin
like I'd been branded.

He called me "baby."
I called him "sir."
And when I left,
I deleted the post
like that could undo what I sold.

But Craigslist has memory.
So do I.

She Left Her Real Name Behind

Her name used to be Emily.
Now it's Raven,
or Star,
or whatever sells faster on a slow night.

She doesn't answer to "Mom" anymore.
Says it's easier
when you forget who you were
before the bruises turned into paychecks
and the moaning became background noise.

She left her name
on a birth certificate
somewhere she can't afford to go back to.
Too many eyes,
too many hands,
too many people
who think a woman is only worth
what she'll do for cash.

She keeps a photo
in her shoe—
creases over her daughter's smile.
Sometimes,
after a rough one,
she kisses the face
with lips that forgot what love tastes like.

I asked her once
if she'd ever go back.

To who she was.
To that name.

She said,
"Emily's dead.
But Raven?
Raven eats."

And that was the end of the conversation.

No Saints on Fifth Street

Fifth Street don't sleep.
It sways.
It sells.
It stinks like desperation
and cheap perfume trying to hide it.

The girls lean on lamp posts
like they're waiting for love,
but they're not.
They're waiting for headlights
and hands with cash.
No one brings roses here—
just rolled-up twenties
and broken promises.

The cops pass by
but they don't stop.
They've seen it too much
or maybe they bought it once
and don't want to face the receipt.

We call each other "bitch"
like it's a compliment.
Smoke menthols between dates.
Share lip gloss, condoms, and trauma.
We laugh hard
and cry quiet.
Always quiet.

A preacher tried to save us once—
stood on the corner with a Bible
and a voice full of thunder.
We let him preach.
We even nodded.
But none of us followed him.
Because saints don't work this block.
And God never tips.

I Couldn't Cry, So I Moaned

I wanted to cry,
but he paid for something else.
So I moaned.
Bit my lip.
Rolled my hips
like I meant it.

He didn't notice my eyes were empty.
Didn't care that my hands shook
when he grabbed my hair
too tight,
too familiar,
like he owned pain
and thought I owed it to him.

I used to cry after.
Not anymore.
Now I just wash up,
count the money,
and wonder how much longer
I can split my soul in half
before there's nothing left to sell.

My first time wasn't this bad.
It was worse.
Because I thought it mattered.
I thought it was love
until he zipped up
and left me with silence

and a wet spot
where my heart used to be.

Now I don't call it anything.
Not sex.
Not work.
Not survival.
Just a moment.
A transaction.
A way to get from this day
to the next
without dying.

I moaned
because crying never paid the rent.

Part IV: Risk It All

The Slot Machine Said My Name

It lit up
like it knew me.
Like it missed me.
Spinning cherries,
bells screaming
like angels on speed.

The slot machine said my name.
Not out loud—
but in the way it blinked
like a lover
calling me home.

I fed it my rent money.
Fed it my last twenty.
Fed it hope
like it was a god
with a metal stomach
and no mercy.

I hit once.
Small payout.
Just enough to believe again.
That's how it works.
It hooks you
with crumbs
and makes you chase cake
you'll never taste.

Three hours later,
I was down
to lint and regret.
The lights didn't care.
The machine didn't say goodbye.
It just sat there,
waiting for the next fool
who thought luck
was love in disguise.

I left without looking back.
But part of me stayed,
spinning.

Losing with Style

I wore my lucky jacket,
the one with the burn hole
and three broken dreams in the pocket.
Slicked back my hair.
Smiled like I owned the damn place.

Walked into that casino
like a king
with a wallet full of lies
and just enough credit
to pretend I still had worth.

Blackjack table.
Dealer had a smirk
like she'd seen too many men
bluffing confidence
and hiding fear
under aftershave.

I hit on sixteen.
Stupid move.
She drew a five.
Laughed without laughing.
Took my last chip
like it belonged to her.
Maybe it did.

It wasn't about winning.
Not really.
It was about **how** I lost—

smooth,
loud,
with a drink in hand
and a story to spin
about how close I came
to making it back.

They call it addiction.
I call it performance.
And baby,
I lose
like it's the only thing
I was ever born to do
with style.

Scratch Tickets and Regret

The gas station clerk knows me by name.
I don't know hers.
But she smiles
like we're friends
while I hand her crumpled bills
for a shot at nothing.

I buy five tickets—
always five.
Like it's a ritual.
Like God's hiding redemption
under silver dust
and cheap hope.

I scratch them slow,
like foreplay.
Corner to corner.
Line by line.
Each number a maybe.
Each word a lie.

"WINNER," it says—
once in a while.
Just enough to keep me breathing.
Ten bucks here.
Free ticket there.
But never enough
to undo the week's mistakes.
Never enough

to pay the rent I already spent
trying to feel lucky.

I throw the losers away
like they're nothing.
But they're not.
They're pieces of a dream
I keep tearing up
just to believe in again
tomorrow.

Regret smells like copper
and scratch dust.
And it never leaves my fingers.

Pawned My Wedding Ring Again

Third time this year.
The guy behind the counter
didn't even ask why.
Just weighed it,
nodded,
and slid me a stack of bills
that looked too small
for what that ring used to mean.

I told myself I'd buy it back.
I always do.
I never do.

It wasn't about her anymore.
Not really.
She's long gone—
took the dishes, the dog,
and the last piece of me
that still believed
in forever.

But that ring?
That ring was proof
I tried.
Once.
Back when love
was louder than debt
and I still believed
I could gamble with time
and win.

Now it's just metal.
Pawnshop shine.
Another sacrifice
for one more spin,
one more bet,
one more second
pretending I'm not losing everything
just to feel alive
for five goddamn minutes.

Roulette Night Prayers

I prayed to the wheel.
Not to God.
Not to saints.
To a spinning blur
of red and black
that didn't care
who I was
or what I'd lost.

I whispered numbers
like scripture.
Seven.
Twelve.
Twenty-three.
My daughter's birthday.
My clean time.
The age I was
before I started lying
to myself for sport.

Each spin felt holy.
Each click a heartbeat.
Each ball drop
a judgment
delivered without mercy
or meaning.

I crossed myself once,
not because I believed,
but because habit

dies harder than hope.
And I was dying
for just one win.

The guy next to me
blew his rent
in three spins.
Laughed like a man
already halfway buried.

I didn't laugh.
I just closed my eyes
and asked the wheel
to give me something—
anything—
that felt like control
in a life
I never really held.

Amen
came in silence.

Bet on Nothing, Got Less

I told myself I wasn't addicted—
I just liked the rush.
Said I could quit
whenever I wanted.
I just never wanted to.

I bet on horses I'd never seen,
teams I didn't follow,
coin flips, scratchers,
even the weather once.
Lost every time.
But the loss felt better
than the nothing I had
before the bet.

That's the trick.
You don't gamble
because you think you'll win.
You gamble
because losing hurts less
than feeling empty.

I once bet my shoes.
Lost them.
Walked home barefoot
like a pilgrim with no god
and blisters for blessings.

When I finally stopped,
I didn't feel clean.

I felt hollow.
Like I'd scraped out my soul
with a poker chip
and left the rest
on a barstool
next to a man
who looked just like me
but smiled more
because he still believed
in luck.

I bet on nothing.
Got less.
And even now,
part of me wonders
if the next hand
would've saved me.

Part V: Rot Beneath the Skin

Therapist's Eyes Look Tired

She blinked slow
like I was just the next storm
on her schedule.
Clipboard in one hand,
sympathy in the other,
but her smile
didn't reach her eyes.

I told her about the nightmares,
about the panic,
about the moments where my own breath
felt like a threat.
She nodded.
Scribbled something.
Probably "trauma."
Probably "noncompliant."
Probably "still broken."

She asked how I felt.
I said "fine,"
because saying anything else
meant unraveling
in front of someone
paid to pretend they care.

I could tell she'd heard it all before.
My story was just another
cracked plate
in her cabinet of broken people.
She wasn't cruel.

She was tired.
And I couldn't blame her.

The hour ended
before the tears started.
She handed me a paper
with breathing exercises
like I hadn't been holding my breath
since I was twelve.

Next appointment:
two weeks out.
Still shaking,
still hollow,
but at least now
I had a name for it.

Cutting Through the Noise

It wasn't about blood.
Not really.
It was about control—
the kind I couldn't find
in bottles,
in pills,
in prayers no one answered.

The world screamed too loud.
Thoughts crashed like glass
in my skull.
So I cut
to quiet them.
To bleed out the chaos
one slice at a time.

No one noticed.
Not at first.
Long sleeves,
fake smiles,
the usual lies.
You learn quick
how to perform "okay."
Even while falling apart
in private.

The first time it scared me.
The second time,
it soothed me.

By the fifth,
I stopped counting.

It wasn't a cry for help.
It was the only way
to feel something
that wasn't screaming.
Something real.
Something mine.

People say "just talk about it."
But talking never silenced the noise.
It just made it echo louder.

The blade didn't lie.
The blade didn't judge.
It just listened.
And sometimes,
that was enough.

Screaming into My Hands

I screamed into my hands
because the walls had ears
and the neighbors
were already tired of the noise.

My hands smelled like metal.
Like fear.
Like the nights I shook
until I couldn't remember
why I started shaking in the first place.

It wasn't a loud scream.
Not the kind that rips the sky.
It was the silent kind—
the one that gets trapped in your throat
and burns like acid.
The kind that turns into migraines
and bad choices.

I'd bite my palm sometimes.
Just to feel.
Just to prove
I still could.

People think breakdowns are dramatic.
Throwing dishes,
crying in the rain.
Mine happened
in the back of a closet
with socks in my mouth

and rage chewing through my chest
like rats in the walls.

I didn't want anyone to hear me.
Because if they did,
they might ask,
"What's wrong?"
And I didn't have the words.
Just the sound.
Buried in my hands.

I Was a Ghost in High School

I walked those halls
like a rumor.
Present,
but never seen.
A shadow between lockers,
a silence in the back row.

Teachers forgot my name.
Called me "him"
or "you"
or just skipped me altogether.
I didn't raise my hand.
Didn't speak.
Didn't want to give them
another reason to look disappointed.

I ate lunch in the bathroom
more times than I'll admit.
The stall was quieter
than a table full of people
who pretended I wasn't real.

No one asked if I was okay.
Maybe I looked too normal.
Maybe I wore the right mask.
Maybe the rot inside
was too quiet
to make a scene.

I didn't go to prom.
Didn't date.
Didn't leave a mark
on anyone's memory.

I graduated like a ghost
drifting across the stage
in a rented robe,
wondering if the paper they handed me
was a death certificate
for the kid I used to be.

Prozac and Pancakes

I took the pill
with day-old coffee
and called it breakfast.
My hands still shook,
but the edges weren't so sharp.
Just dull enough
to get through the morning
without bleeding on anyone.

Prozac and pancakes—
the Sunday ritual.
Mom made them
like things were normal,
like I wasn't one skipped dose away
from unraveling at the table.

She didn't ask
if I felt better.
She just added more syrup.
Like sugar could soak up
the sadness
settling in my chest
like wet cement.

The meds made me slow.
Not peaceful—
just muted.
Like someone turned down the volume
on everything I used to feel.

I missed my sadness,
some days.
At least it felt honest.
At least it was mine.

But I kept taking the pills,
because not taking them
was worse.
Because pancakes
weren't enough
to make me want
to stay.

Suicide Notes I Never Wrote

There were so many.
Unwritten,
unfinished,
folded in the back of my brain
like napkins soaked in blood.

I'd plan them
in the shower,
on long drives,
while standing at the edge
of nothing in particular.

"It's not your fault."
"I just got tired."
"Please remember me better than I was."

None of it felt honest.
What I really wanted to say
was:
"I don't know how to live like this anymore."
"I'm so fucking tired of pretending."
"It hurts, even when it doesn't."

But I never wrote them.
Because writing them down
made it real.
And I wasn't sure
if I wanted goodbye
or just attention

from someone who wouldn't flinch
at the mess I'd become.

Instead,
I smoked.
I drank.
I stayed alive
out of spite
or stubbornness
or maybe
just because I didn't want my mother
to find the body.

Some days,
that was enough.
Some days,
barely.

Part VI: Ashes & Embers

Scars Make Terrible Maps

I tried to trace my life
through the scars.
Thought maybe they'd tell me
where I'd been,
what I'd survived,
why I still wake up
even when I don't want to.

But scars don't give directions.
They just mark the places
you bled
and didn't die.

There's one on my arm
from the night I slammed a window
instead of my own skull.
One on my ankle
from running barefoot
away from someone
who said they loved me
but hit like they hated themselves.

I've got scars on the inside, too.
On parts of me
no one ever sees.
Memories that scratch
like rusted nails
in the quiet hours.
Words I believed
long after they stopped being said.

People look at scars
like proof of strength.
But some are just evidence—
receipts for pain
I never asked to feel.

I stopped trying to map them.
I just live with them.
Like reminders.
Like ghosts.
Like skin that learned
to grow back wrong.

Woke Up Sober, Stayed That Way

I woke up sober
and didn't know what to do
with all the noise.

No hangover fog
to blur the guilt.
No high
to soften the truth.
Just morning,
loud and honest
and ugly.

My hands shook.
Not from withdrawal—
from memory.
From realizing I couldn't run
to the bottle,
the pill,
the needle,
the bed of someone
who never asked my name.

I stared at the ceiling
for an hour,
counting reasons
not to use.
Some were real.
Some were lies
I told myself

because the truth was too small
to stand on.

Coffee tasted bitter.
My clothes didn't fit right.
My skin itched
like it missed the poison.

But I didn't reach for it.
Not that day.
Not even when the silence
got too heavy
and my shadow whispered
just one
just once.

I stayed sober.
Not because I wanted to.
Because I didn't want to start
again.

And sometimes,
that's enough.

The Girl Who Didn't Die

They called it a miracle.
Said she was lucky.
Said someone up there
must've had a plan.

She just laughed.
The kind of laugh
that tastes like rust.
Because it wasn't a miracle.
It was a missed vein,
a locked door,
a half-second pause
before the rope pulled tight.

She didn't die.
But part of her did.
The soft part.
The part that wrote poems
about stars
and believed people meant what they said.

Now she walks
like a shadow
that forgot how to reach
for light.
Talks in half-sentences
and flinches when people say
"You're so strong."

They don't see the pills
she lines up every morning
like soldiers.
Don't hear the way she screams
into her pillow
when the silence
gets too sharp.

She didn't die.
And that's supposed to be enough.
But some days,
she wonders
if surviving
was just a longer way
to fall.

I Don't Believe in Hope, But I Use It

Hope's a scam.
A cheap high
wrapped in Hallmark slogans
and Instagram quotes
about light
and healing
and shit that never worked for me.

I don't believe in it.
Not really.
But I use it.
Like duct tape
on a soul that's splitting open.

Sometimes,
it's just getting out of bed.
Brushing my teeth.
Answering a text
without lying.
Tiny things.
Stupid things.
But they matter
more than I want to admit.

I've seen too much
to believe in miracles.
Too many funerals.
Too many friends
who folded under the weight
of one more day.

But I still check the sky
for no reason.
Still put on clean clothes
even when I'm not leaving the house.
Still whisper "maybe"
on the days
when "never" feels easier to say.

Hope's not light.
It's friction.
A spark
in the dark
that hurts your eyes
but keeps you from disappearing.

I don't believe in hope.
But I carry it
like a blade.
Just in case.

Healing Is Boring

No one tells you
how boring healing is.

No chaos.
No drama.
Just waking up
on time,
taking your meds,
brushing your teeth,
doing the laundry
before it smells like regret.

I used to burn bright—
drunk at midnight,
crying on rooftops,
running from lovers
and toward oblivion
like it owed me something.

Now I make grocery lists.
Pay bills.
Cancel plans
because I'm tired,
not because I'm high.

Healing isn't loud.
It's quiet.
Like waiting in line
at the pharmacy.
Like saying no

when every bone in your body
wants to scream yes.

Some days,
I miss the fire.
Miss the rush,
the ruin,
the way falling apart
felt like flying
for one brief second.

But this—
this stillness,
this boring peace—
it's mine.
And I've bled enough
to earn it.

Today Was Quiet and That's Enough

No panic.
No phone calls.
No shaking hands
trying to find something to hold
that won't break me.

Just quiet.
Just coffee that didn't spill.
Just a sky that didn't fall.
Just a breath
I didn't have to fight for.

I didn't cry today.
Didn't scream into the sink.
Didn't stare too long at the pills
and wonder what if.

I didn't feel happy.
But I didn't feel lost either.
And maybe that's something.
Maybe that's progress
in its smallest,
most ordinary form.

I made a sandwich.
Watched a stupid show.
Laughed once—
not loud,
but real.

No miracles.
No revelations.
Just a day
without drowning.

Tomorrow might come with teeth.
Might tear me open again.
But today
was quiet.

And that's enough.

Part VII: No Fixed Address

Shelter Smells Like Desperation

Smells like sweat
and socks that gave up last week.
Like microwaved noodles
and stale breath
and wet cardboard
masquerading as dignity.

The air is heavy
with stories no one asked to carry.
A man mutters in his sleep
about a brother he buried.
A woman hums to herself
like the song might keep
the ghosts away.

There are rules—
lights out at ten,
no fights,
no drugs,
no hope strong enough
to get you kicked out.

Cots line the room
like coffins waiting for their turn.
You don't sleep.
You hover.
You flinch when footsteps get too close
and you keep your shoes on
just in case.

You learn quick
to guard your blanket,
guard your bag,
guard your name
like someone might steal
the last piece of you
that still feels human.

It's not a shelter.
It's a pause.
A breath
between drowning
and going under again.

Cardboard and Concrete

Cardboard don't keep out the cold,
but it gives you something
to pretend with.
Pretend it's a wall.
Pretend it's a bed.
Pretend it's not
just garbage between you
and the concrete
that knows your name
better than your own mother does.

Concrete remembers your bones.
Knows the way your spine curves
when you sleep on it too long.
It doesn't judge.
It just takes.

You fold cardboard like prayers.
Layer it like skin.
Lay it down like a lie
you almost believe.
"This is fine."
"I'll be okay."
"It's just for tonight."

But nights stretch.
They don't end.
They just bleed into mornings
that look the same
as the one before—

empty coffee cup,
dirty shoes,
a bus you can't afford
to chase.

Cardboard and concrete
don't give answers.
They just wait
for you to disappear quietly.

And most nights,
you almost do.

Nobody Looks at You

You could be bleeding
on the sidewalk,
shirt torn,
eyes wild,
and still—
they wouldn't look.

They glance
then glance away,
like your pain
might be contagious
if they hold your stare too long.

Mothers pull their kids closer.
Teenagers laugh
but never stop walking.
Businessmen check their phones
like that screen
can shield them from guilt.

You stop being a person.
Start being a stain,
a shape,
a warning.
Something they step around
like a crack
in the concrete
they're too good to fall into.

You talk to yourself
just to hear a voice.
Doesn't matter if it's yours.
Doesn't matter if it makes sense.
You just need to remember
you still exist.

And when someone
finally does make eye contact—
a second,
just a second—
it hits like sunlight
through a boarded-up window.

Nobody looks at you.
And that's how you vanish
before you're even gone.

My Zip Code Was a Park Bench

That bench knew my name.
Knew the weight of my back,
the angle of my knees,
the sound I made
when dreams fell out of my mouth
in my sleep.

It faced the road,
so I could pretend
I was just resting,
just thinking,
just another soul
watching the world
instead of someone
the world forgot.

Rain turned it slick.
Sun made it a skillet.
Winter made it stone.
But it was mine.
More honest
than any door
that ever locked behind me.

Cops came around
and told me to move.
I asked,
"To where?"
They didn't answer.
Just gave me that look—

the one that says
"You're not supposed to be here."
But I was.
Every night.
Me and the bench
and the plastic bag of everything I owned.

I memorized the cracks in the sidewalk
like addresses.
My zip code was silence.
My city was shame.

But that bench—
that bench
was home
when nothing else would have me.

Showers Cost $5 at the Truck Stop

It's five bucks
for ten minutes of steam
and the chance
to feel like a human being again.

You wait in line
with truckers,
drifters,
and people who've forgotten
what it's like
to be clean on the inside.

The water's always too hot.
Burns the dirt off
but not the weight.
Not the guilt.
Not the stink of survival
you wear like a second skin.

You scrub hard—
armpits,
feet,
soul if you could reach it.
Watch the grime swirl down
like proof
you still exist.

No one looks you in the eye.
Not here.
Not anywhere.

You keep your head down,
soap in your pocket,
towel borrowed
from the shelter
that won't remember your name.

When it's over,
you dry off fast,
step back into clothes
that still smell like the street,
and walk out
with wet hair
and five dollars less
but almost enough dignity
to make it through another day.

Home Is a Word I Forgot

I used to say "I'm going home"
without thinking.
Just a word.
A place.
A light left on.

Now it feels foreign,
like a language
I never learned to speak.

Home isn't four walls.
It's safety.
It's silence that doesn't hurt.
It's knowing
no one's going to kick you out
if you fall apart
on the kitchen floor.

I've slept in doorways,
under bridges,
behind dumpsters
that smelled like the truth.
I've curled up
on library steps
with a hoodie for a blanket
and my shoes under my head
so they wouldn't get stolen.

People say,
"You can always come home."

But they don't mean it.
Not if you smell like rain and rot.
Not if your voice cracks
from asking too many times
for too little.

Home is a word I forgot.
And maybe that's for the best.
Because forgetting
hurts less
than remembering
what it used to mean.

Part VIII: Choices and Consequences

The Clinic Was Too Quiet

No one talks above a whisper
in the waiting room.
Not even the ones
pretending it's just another check-up.
Just another Tuesday.

The clock ticks loud,
like it's judging.
Like it knows
what we're all here for.

The chairs are cold.
The air smells like bleach
and pretending.
Eyes stay on magazines,
walls,
floors—
anywhere but each other.

When they called my name,
I stood like my legs didn't want to.
Like they knew
I was walking toward a decision
I'd carry in my spine
for the rest of my life.

The nurse was kind.
Too kind.
That kind of voice you use
when someone's breaking
but still pretending not to be.

The hallway was quiet.
The room was colder.
And when it was over,
I didn't cry.
Not there.
Not in front of the nurse
who patted my shoulder
like she was afraid
I'd dissolve.

But when I got outside,
the sky felt too big.
Too bright.
Too loud.

And I couldn't hear
anything
but my own heartbeat
and the silence
I had just bought.

I Named Her Anyway

I never held her.
Never kissed her forehead.
Never counted fingers or toes.
But I named her anyway.
Because something inside me
needed to.

"Mara."
It means bitterness.
It means strength.
It means a name I can whisper
when the guilt creeps in
at 2 a.m.
and nothing can quiet it
but memory
and maybe grace.

I never told anyone.
Not even him.
He didn't ask.
He just drove me to the clinic,
smoked a cigarette while I signed the forms,
and said
"You sure about this?"
as if anything was sure
in that moment.

I said yes.
Because no
was too heavy.

Because love
shouldn't feel like a trap
with a heartbeat.
Because I was already drowning
and she deserved more
than a mother
with nothing to give.

Sometimes I wonder
what she'd look like.
If her laugh would sound
like mine
or like the one I used to have
before life
started asking too much.

I never met her.
But she lives
in the quiet corners
of my prayers
even now.
Even still.

The Protester Called Me Murderer

He held a sign
with a photo of a fetus
and eyes like fire
burning holes
through my coat.

"Murderer,"
he said.
Like he knew me.
Like he'd sat in the dark
with my rent past due,
my fridge empty,
my hands shaking
because I hadn't eaten
in two days.

He didn't see the bruises.
Didn't ask who put them there.
Didn't know that the baby
wasn't made in love—
but in silence,
and force,
and a locked door
that still echoes
when I close my eyes.

He called it life.
But what about mine?
What about waking up
in a world

that punishes women
for surviving
the things men pretend
not to do?

I walked past him,
eyes forward,
heart loud.
He spit the word again—
"Murderer."
And I almost turned around.
Almost told him
he was too late.

Because I already
killed the part of me
that believed
I deserved to choose.

Two Lines on the Test

Two lines.
One moment.
Everything changed.

The test sat on the bathroom sink
like a verdict.
No jury.
No appeal.
Just two pink lines
and a silence
that screamed.

I stared at it
like it might blink.
Like maybe it was wrong.
Like maybe my body
was just confused—
like me.

I thought about names.
Then I thought about rent.
Then I thought about
how I couldn't even remember
the last time I felt
safe.
Whole.
Capable.

I texted him.
He didn't answer.

Called twice.
Voicemail.
Figures.

The mirror showed a woman
I barely recognized—
skin pale,
lips cracked,
eyes full of war
with no weapon
but choice.

Two lines
aren't just lines.
They're weight.
They're futures.
They're the kind of math
that never adds up
no matter how many times
you try to solve it.

I threw the test away.
But it didn't leave me.
It still shows up
in dreams,
in memories,
in moments
when I wonder
what could've been
if I had more
than fear
and two lines.

I Didn't Want to Be a Mother

I didn't want to be a mother.
Not then.
Not like that.
Not with a man
who said he loved me
but never once asked
if I was okay.

The world doesn't like
when women say that out loud.
They want us glowing,
grateful,
ready to break ourselves
into pieces
for something
we didn't ask for.

But I knew—
deep down,
bone-deep—
that I couldn't do it.
Not with no job,
no help,
no hope.
Not with trauma still fresh
like a wound I kept licking
just to feel alive.

They say motherhood is instinct.
But survival is, too.

And that's what I chose.
Not because I hated her.
But because I couldn't
drag her through the fire
I was still burning in.

I didn't want to be a mother.
And maybe that makes me selfish.
But selfish
is what kept me breathing.
And breathing
was all I could manage.

God, Forgive Me or Don't

I didn't light a candle.
Didn't kneel.
Didn't whisper some pretty prayer
to a sky
that's never once answered me back.

I just stood there—
in a bathroom stall
at the clinic,
staring at my shaking hands
like they belonged
to someone else.

They say God forgives everything.
But what if I don't want forgiveness?
What if I'm too tired
to feel sorry
for surviving
the only way I knew how?

I didn't do it out of hate.
I did it
because I had nothing left to give.
Because love,
real love,
means knowing
when you'd destroy someone
just by holding on.

I thought maybe I'd feel something—
relief,
guilt,
grief.
But all I felt
was empty
in a way that was
almost peaceful.

So, God,
if You're listening—
forgive me.
Or don't.
I'm done begging for mercy
from someone
who watched me break
and never once
reached out a hand.

Part IX: Behind Closed Doors

Bruises Are Love Notes Now

He never says sorry.
He says,
"Look what you made me do."
Then buys flowers.
Then takes me to bed.
Then hits repeat.

The first time,
I cried.
The second time,
I told myself it was stress.
By the fifth,
I started wearing long sleeves
even in summer.

The bruises bloomed like ink—
purple apologies
written across my arms,
my thighs,
my ribs.
Love notes,
he called them once,
laughing like it was a joke
and I was supposed to be in on it.

I stayed.
Because leaving felt harder.
Because no one believed me
the first time I said
I wasn't safe.

Because the world loves a man
who knows how to smile in public
and destroy in private.

He kisses my forehead
like a brand.
Whispers **"I love you"**
after he breaks me.
And I believe it
just long enough
to let him do it again.

Bruises fade.
But the echo stays.

And some nights,
it's the only thing
I can still feel.

He Said He'd Change

He said he'd change
with tears in his eyes
and blood on his knuckles.
Said it like a vow,
like a promise made under pressure
and fear
and the weight of everything
he broke.

I wanted to believe him.
Wanted it so bad
I held my breath
every time he reached for me
without fists.

He cleaned the house.
Bought groceries.
Made love like an apology
he didn't know how to say
any other way.

And for a week,
maybe two,
I thought maybe love
was enough.

But change doesn't come
with flowers.
It doesn't arrive
in the quiet between storms.

It takes work.
And work was something
he never did
unless it was rebuilding the lie
he swore
was the last one.

The next time he hit me,
he didn't even cry.
He just smoked a cigarette
and asked what I wanted
for dinner.

And I realized—
he never planned to change.
He just wanted me
to stay.

The Neighbors Heard, Said Nothing

The walls were thin.
Everyone knew it.
You could hear the dog bark
three doors down,
the couple upstairs fighting
about rent and cigarettes.
So I know they heard me.
All of them.

The crash of glass.
The thud of my body
against the dresser.
My voice breaking
as I begged him to stop
in a tone
that wasn't anger
but survival.

The baby next door cried.
The TV next window over got louder.
Someone closed their blinds
like that could keep the guilt out.

They heard it.
They had to.
My screams weren't small.
My silence after
was louder.

But no one came.
No knock.
No call.
No help.
Just a hallway full of locked doors
and neighbors
who learned to sleep through violence
as long as it wasn't their own.

They saw the bruises,
pretended not to.
Gave tight smiles in passing
like I was contagious.

The worst part wasn't the beating.
It was knowing
the people around me
chose comfort
over courage.

My Daughter Hid Under the Sink

She was five,
too small to understand,
but old enough to know
where to hide
when the shouting started.

I found her curled up
under the kitchen sink,
arms around her knees,
a stuffed rabbit pressed tight
against her chest
like it could absorb
the fear in her bones.

She didn't cry.
She whispered,
"Is it over?"
like it was a storm
we were waiting to pass
instead of a man
we let stay.

I told her yes.
Because lying
felt kinder than truth.
Because children shouldn't know
that monsters don't live
under the bed—
they live in the hallway,
in the living room,

in the hands of people
who say they love you.

That night,
I washed the blood off my lip
in silence.
Sat beside her
while she pretended to sleep,
twitching
every time the floor creaked.

I should've left.
But I didn't.
Because fear
is a chain
that hugs you tight.

And shame
makes you believe
you deserve the bruises
and the silence
and the sound of your child
learning how to disappear.

Why I Flinched When You Raised Your Hand

It wasn't your fault.
You were reaching for the remote,
or maybe brushing hair from my face.
You didn't mean it.
But I still flinched
like I was about to break.

Because hands remember.
Even when the moment is soft,
my body still thinks
it's about to get hit.

Muscle doesn't forget
what fear taught it.
The twitch,
the brace,
the shallow breath
before the blow.

I saw your eyes—
how they cracked
when I pulled away.
You didn't ask,
but I saw the question
dripping from your silence.

This is why.
Because love came with fists.
Because "I'm sorry"
meant nothing

after the third time.
Because kindness now
doesn't erase
the violence before.

I'm trying.
I really am.
To trust,
to breathe,
to let hands near me
without counting down.

But healing doesn't come
with a deadline.
And sometimes,
even gentle hands
feel like ghosts
wearing the ones
that hurt me.

Escape in a Grocery Bag

I packed my life
into a grocery bag.
Not a suitcase.
Not a plan.
Just one plastic bag
with a cracked handle
and everything I could grab
while he was in the shower.

A shirt,
my ID,
thirty-seven dollars,
and the photo of my daughter
from kindergarten—
the one with her missing tooth
and her eyes still bright.

I didn't take the ring.
Didn't take the dishes
or the excuses
or the apology letters
he never meant.

I walked fast.
Didn't run.
Running looks suspicious.
Running makes people ask questions.
Walking is quieter,
like you're just going to the corner store,
like you'll be back.

I wasn't going back.

The air felt heavier outside,
but freer.
Like it knew
how long I'd been waiting
to breathe.

No goodbye note.
No revenge.
No drama.

Just a grocery bag
filled with the pieces
of a woman
finally deciding
she didn't have to die
for someone else's anger.

Part X: Left Behind

My Father Was a Ghost Before He Left

He was there—
technically.
His boots by the door,
his breath heavy with beer,
his silence
thick enough to choke on.

But he wasn't there.
Not in the ways that mattered.
Not when I scraped my knees
or brought home a bad grade
or cried myself into a headache
no one noticed.

He sat on the couch
like it was a throne
and the rest of us
were just background noise.
Flicking through channels,
flicking through years,
never once
looking up
to see the people
he forgot how to love.

He left one day—
no warning,
no bags,
no goodbye.
Just gone.

And somehow
that felt more honest
than all the years
he spent pretending to stay.

People asked if I missed him.
How do you miss a shadow?
How do you grieve
what was never truly given?

He was a ghost
long before the door closed.
And I've been haunted
ever since.

No One Came to the Recital

I wore a dress
that itched at the collar
and shoes two sizes too tight
because Mom said
"You look beautiful, baby."
And I wanted to believe her.

I practiced for weeks.
Piano keys,
clumsy fingers,
silent counting under breath.
I got the song right
three times in a row
the night before.

They said they'd come.
They always said.
Dad mumbled something
with a beer in hand.
Mom smiled too wide
like she already knew
it was a lie.

The folding chairs were filled
with other people's families—
clapping,
cheering,
smiling like they meant it.

Mine?
Empty seats
in the second row.
I saved them anyway.
Stared at them
through the whole song
like maybe if I looked hard enough,
they'd appear.

They didn't.

The applause still stung
like pity wrapped in sound.
A teacher patted my back.
Said I did great.
I nodded.
Said thank you.
Tried not to cry
until the hallway
was empty.

No one came to the recital.
But I still played.
Because some part of me
still hoped they'd hear it
from wherever they were.

Raised by TV and Hunger

The TV taught me
how to talk,
how to laugh at things
that weren't funny,
how to wait for something
that never comes.

Cartoons in the morning,
game shows at noon,
dramas at night
while my stomach growled
like it knew something
I didn't.

Mom slept all day.
Or maybe she was passed out.
Hard to tell the difference
when the pills
make her eyes
look like windows
with the lights turned off.

I made dinner
with a microwave
and whatever was left
in dented cans
and expired boxes.
Ramen,
dry cereal,

ketchup sandwiches
if I was lucky.

Nobody tucked me in.
Nobody asked how school was.
Nobody noticed
when I stopped going.

But the TV was always there.
Bright and loud and stupid.
A fake family
with canned laughter
and problems
that solved themselves
in thirty minutes or less.

I watched them eat dinner together
every night
while I scraped the jar
for the last spoon of peanut butter
and pretended
I wasn't starving
for more than food.

I Was Always the One Chasing

I was the one
sending the first text,
making the call,
knocking on doors
that were already closing.

I chased my dad
through voicemail messages
and promises
that faded faster
than the sound of his truck
leaving the driveway.

I chased friends
who only called
when they needed something—
a ride,
a lie,
a piece of me
I didn't have the strength to give
but gave anyway.

I chased love
like it was a bus
I kept missing
by seconds.
Panting.
Hopeful.
Heart bruised from running.

No one ever chased me back.
Not once.
Not when I broke.
Not when I begged.
Not when I stopped showing up
just to see
if anyone noticed.

They didn't.

Now I don't run.
I walk.
Alone.
And if someone wants me—
really wants me—
they can chase
for once.

Goodbye Wasn't Even a Word

He didn't say goodbye.
Didn't pack a bag
or leave a note.
Just vanished
like smoke from a cigarette
he never finished.

One day he was there—
slamming cupboards,
cursing the rent,
breathing too loud.
The next,
his chair stayed empty
like it had been waiting
for silence all along.

I waited,
at first.
Thought maybe he'd call.
Maybe he got lost,
or scared,
or sobered up
and needed space.

But space turns into distance.
Distance into forgetting.
And forgetting—
that's where he excelled.

Goodbye wasn't a word
in his vocabulary.
It was a shrug,
a slammed door,
an echo that didn't care
what it left behind.

And me?
I stopped asking why.
Stopped expecting closure.
Because sometimes
you don't get an ending—
just absence
where love should have been.

The Couch Where I Waited

It was brown
and sunken in the middle,
springs poking like questions
no one wanted to answer.

That couch knew my weight.
Knew the shape I made
when I sat still
for hours—
waiting for a knock,
a phone call,
a voice
that never came.

I used to count cars
through the window,
hoping one would slow down,
pull in,
mean something.

It never did.

Sometimes I'd rehearse
what I'd say—
"Where were you?"
"Why'd you leave?"
"Did you even think about me?"
But the answers
never came either.
Just the TV's hum,

a flickering lamp,
and the ache
of being forgotten
in plain sight.

The couch sagged more each year.
Like it was tired too.
Like it had absorbed
every second
of waiting
and disappointment.

I don't sit there anymore.
But I still see it
in dreams.
Still feel the shape
of longing
etched into its cushions.

Still remember
what it felt like
to hope
and not be enough.

Part XI: Caged Lives

Visitation Through Plexiglass

They sat me in a chair
across from a wall of glass,
scratched and smudged
like every promise
he ever made.

He picked up the phone
with shaking hands.
So did I.
Plastic to plastic,
no touch.
Just words
filtered through static
and years we lost
to bad choices
and barbed wire.

He looked older.
Paler.
Eyes like someone
who hadn't seen sky in months.
I wanted to ask him
if he still dreamed,
if the cell was cold,
if he thought about Mom
or me
or the things we didn't say
before the sirens came.

But I just said,
"Hi."
And he just nodded,
like that was all we had left.

There's something cruel
about glass you can't break
between people
who already did.

The guard said,
"Five minutes."
So we wasted three
just looking at each other—
trying to remember
what it felt like
to be free
at the same time.

Number, Not a Name

They took his name
the second he walked in.
Replaced it with seven digits
and a jumpsuit
that didn't fit.

He used to be Marcus.
Now he's **#4672983.**
Roll call,
head count,
no one says it with feeling.
Just noise
in a building full of ghosts
wearing skin.

In here,
you're not someone's son,
someone's father,
someone's maybe.
You're just a number
in a broken machine
that swallows men
and spits them out
with more scars
than chances.

They say he pled guilty.
I say he pled tired.
Tired of fighting,
tired of losing,

tired of being the villain
in a story no one asked
why he ended up in.

He told me once,
**"They don't call you anything
they don't plan to throw away."**
And I felt that
in my chest.
Like a truth
too heavy to carry,
too real to drop.

He's still Marcus to me.
Even if they never
say his name again.

23 Hours a Day

Twenty-three hours
in a concrete box
with a toilet
and a bed
and thoughts
that don't stop.

One hour out.
If they feel like it.
If nothing goes wrong.
If you keep your mouth shut
and your fists in your pockets.

Time stretches here.
Not like rubber—
like wire.
Tight.
Sharp.
Unforgiving.

You count cracks in the wall.
Count breath.
Count regrets
like beads on a rosary
you stopped believing in.

No clocks.
No mirrors.
Just a fluorescent sun
that never sets

and dreams
you forget on purpose.

You learn how to disappear
without dying.
How to fold into silence
and still hear everything
that's not being said.

They call it **"segregation."**
I call it
"practice for the grave."

But some of us
make it out.
Not better.
Just breathing.

And sometimes
that's enough
to call it survival.

Prison Letters from My Brother

They come once a month,
handwritten in blocky letters
on paper that smells like dust
and distance.

He starts every one with
"I'm doing okay."
I know he's lying.
But I circle the words anyway,
like they're prayers
trying to get out.

He doesn't ask for money.
Doesn't ask for anything
except pictures—
old ones,
good ones,
the kind that don't remind him
how long he's been gone.

He tells me about chow,
the fights,
the books he's reading.
Tells me he's learning to paint
on cardboard
with brushes made from toothbrushes
and hope.

He signs each letter
"Love always, your brother."

Like that love
has weight
strong enough
to reach through cinder blocks
and steel bars.

I keep his letters in a shoebox.
They bend at the edges,
smudged with time.
I read them
when the world feels too clean,
too free,
too unaware
of who we've locked away
and called monsters
because we forgot
they were just boys
once.

Parole Was a Lie

They said he was free.
Parole granted.
Time served.
Go build a life again.

But freedom
with a leash
ain't freedom.
It's just a longer chain
with a smile stitched on.

They watch you—
every step,
every job application,
every piss test
that turns your body
into evidence.

He couldn't rent an apartment.
Couldn't get a job
that paid more than crumbs.
Couldn't breathe
without a system
checking the pulse.

The officer called it structure.
He called it hell
with paperwork.

The world said,
"You got another chance."

But all they gave him
was a narrow hallway
with locked doors
on both sides.

One wrong move
and they'd drag him back.
No questions.
No time to explain.
Just sirens
and cuffs
and that same cold cell
with his name still scratched
on the wall.

Parole was a lie.
A performance
they made him audition for
again
and again.

And when he finally stopped trying,
they said,
"See? We knew he'd fail."

Released But Still Locked In

He walked out
into air that didn't smell
like bleach and concrete.
No guards.
No bars.
No numbers on his chest.
Just sky—
too wide,
too blue,
too unfamiliar.

People said,
"Welcome home."
But where was that?
His bed was a couch.
His past—
a jacket he couldn't take off.
Everyone saw it.
Even when he tried to smile.

He jumped at loud noises.
A slammed door.
A phone ringing.
He ate fast,
eyes darting
like someone might take the meal
mid-bite.

Job interviews
turned cold

when they read his record.
Second chances
sound nice
until they see who they're for.

He said the worst part
was the silence.
The way no one asked
how it felt
to come back
and still feel caged
by every look,
every label,
every locked door
with a polite sign that read:
"We're not hiring."

He was released.
But the bars followed.
Different shape.
Same sentence.

Part XII: Mourning That Won't End

She Died on a Wednesday

She died on a Wednesday.
The kind of day
no one remembers.
Clouds like wet cotton,
air too still,
time ticking
like it forgot how to move.

The nurse said it was peaceful.
That's what they always say.
Like dying quietly
makes it easier to survive.

I sat in the chair beside her bed,
holding a hand
that used to hold mine
when I was small
and scared
and thought she could fix everything.

But death
doesn't care about memories.
Doesn't care about unfinished apologies
or birthday cards
never sent.

I wanted to scream.
Break something.
Shake her awake
and tell her I wasn't ready

to carry the weight
of all her silences.

But I didn't.
I just sat there.
Counting the seconds
after her last breath.
As if time could be rewound
if I paid attention
hard enough.

She died on a Wednesday.
And every Wednesday since
has felt
just a little
too quiet.

I Still Set a Place for Her

Every year on her birthday,
I set a plate,
pour her coffee,
put the sugar in first
just like she did.
No milk.
No talking.
Just silence
where her laugh used to live.

It's stupid, maybe.
Crazy, some would say.
But grief makes rituals
out of survival.
And I need something
to hold on to
when everything else
slips through my fingers
like ash.

I talk to the chair.
Not much.
Just a few words,
like she might answer
if the wind listens right.

I tell her I'm okay.
That I'm still breathing.
That I remember
how she used to hum

when she folded laundry
and how she smelled
like soap and sadness.

The coffee goes cold.
The plate stays full.
But the place is there—
a sacred emptiness
I refuse to fill.

Because if I stop setting it,
if I stop pretending
she's still here,
then maybe she really is gone.

And I'm not ready
to live in a world
where she doesn't exist
at least
for one meal.

My Son's Shoes by the Door

I still trip over them sometimes.
The scuffed sneakers,
laces knotted tight
like he was always
ready to run.

They sit where he left them—
by the door,
to the left,
under the hook
where his jacket used to hang.
Like he's just out for a minute,
just late coming home,
just
not gone.

I tried to put them away once.
Held them in both hands
and shook
like the floor might open
if I let them go.

They still smell like him.
Grass.
Sweat.
Bubble gum.
Childhood wrapped in rubber soles
and dirt
from a field he'll never play on again.

People say,
"It's time to move on."
But move where?
To what?
Grief built this house.
And his shoes
are the only thing that still feels
like proof
he was here.

I'd rather trip
a hundred more times
than wake up
in a world
where those shoes
aren't waiting
by the door.

Grief Spoke in Tongues

Grief didn't speak English.
It didn't speak at all.
Just moaned
through the walls at night,
rattled my chest
like a language made of sobs
and silence.

It said everything
without saying a word—
through broken plates,
missed calls,
a sink full of dishes
I stopped pretending to clean.

It spoke in headaches
and songs I couldn't finish.
In coffee gone cold
three mornings in a row.
In the way I stared at the TV
without seeing
anything.

People offered comfort
like phrases from a script—
"They're in a better place."
"Time heals."
"At least you had them."
But those words
felt like someone trying to read

from the wrong page
of the wrong book
in a language
they never had to learn.

Grief taught me fluency
in what's left behind.
In empty rooms.
In birthdays that ache.
In talking to the air
like it might talk back.

And when I finally spoke,
it wasn't loud.
It wasn't pretty.
But it was mine.

I Don't Cry, I Break Things

I don't cry.
Not the way people want me to.
Not the soft, wet sadness
with tissues
and whispered prayers.

I slam doors.
I punch walls.
I throw glasses at the sink
like maybe the shatter
can say what I can't.

Grief comes out
like fire in my chest.
Like rage in my hands.
Like fury
at a world that took
and didn't give back.

I don't sob.
I crack.
Loud.
Ugly.
Unapologetic.

They say I need to process.
To let it out.
But what if it's not tears
I'm made of?
What if the only way

I know how to mourn
is with blood on my knuckles
and apologies
I never say?

I don't cry.
Not because I don't miss them.
But because crying
feels like surrender.
And I've lost too much already
to give grief
one more thing.

So I break things.
Because something
has to break
when the heart can't.

The Last Picture of My Mother

It was in my wallet
for ten years.
Her hair pinned back,
smiling like she believed in something.
I used to trace her face with my thumb
whenever I got too far gone.

That picture made it through
eviction,
jail,
cold nights in the back of a Buick
with a broken heater
and a stolen blanket.

Then one day,
I traded it.
Just like that.
A guy had half a gram
and no heart.
I had no shame.

It wasn't even a hard choice.
That's the worst part.
I didn't hesitate.
Didn't blink.
Didn't whisper "sorry, Mom."

I walked away
with blood on my sleeve

and a vein singing
like it missed me.

Later,
I looked for that picture
in my mind,
but it was gone—
blurred out
like the rest of my reasons
for getting clean.

All I remember now
is that she smiled
like she knew
I wouldn't make it.

Part XIII: Things I'll Never Say Out Loud

I Faked the Smile at Graduation

They called my name
and everyone clapped
like they knew
how hard I worked.
Like they thought
I had made it.

But I was barely holding it together.
The cap felt too tight.
The gown smelled like sweat
and borrowed pride.
And my smile—
that smile—
was stitched on
with the same thread
that kept my life
from falling apart completely.

No one saw
the skipped meals,
the panic attacks,
the nights I stared at the ceiling
wondering if the diploma
was worth the pieces of me
I lost getting it.

No one knew
I'd been high during finals,
crying in the library bathroom,
writing papers I wouldn't remember

because the alternative
was disappearing.

They took pictures.
Told me to smile bigger.
Told me I looked so happy.
But happiness isn't what I wore that day.
It was survival.
It was exhaustion
dressed in black and gold.

I faked the smile.
Because no one wants the truth
in a graduation photo.

What Happened at Uncle Rick's

I was nine.
Too old to be fooled,
too young to know
how to fight back.

He smelled like beer
and something sour
when he pulled me close
and said
"It's our little secret."
I didn't even know
what I was supposed to be
keeping secret.

The room was dark.
The TV was still on.
Cartoons with the sound turned low
so no one would hear
what wasn't supposed to happen.

I told my mom
he touched me.
She told me
I misunderstood.
Said he wouldn't do that.
Said I shouldn't lie
about family.

So I didn't.
Not again.

I learned how to shut up.
How to bury it
under fake smiles
and changed clothes
and a silence
so loud
it still rings in my ears
when someone says
"Tell me about your childhood."

What happened at Uncle Rick's
wasn't just that night.
It was every night after
I didn't feel safe
in my own skin.

And I still don't.

I Hate My Reflection

I avoid mirrors.
Not because I'm vain,
but because they show me
too much.
The curve of my shame.
The slope of every failure
etched into my posture.
Eyes that flinch
like they expect the slap.

People say self-love starts with acceptance.
But what do you do
when the face staring back
reminds you
of every time you stayed quiet
when you should've screamed?

I see scars
no one else can.
The ones under the skin.
The ones shaped like names
I wish I never learned
to whisper.

Sometimes I try to smile at myself.
It feels like lying.
Like wearing clothes
that don't belong to me.

I hate the way I look
because it proves
I'm still here.
That I survived
what should've broken me—
but didn't fix me either.

I want to love this face.
Really, I do.
But most days,
I just look away
and pretend
it isn't mine.

The Closet Still Smells Like 2006

The carpet's been replaced.
The paint is fresh.
But when I open the door,
it still smells like 2006—
like fear,
and sweat,
and silence too loud to scream through.

That's where I hid
when the shouting started.
When fists flew
and dishes shattered
like promises
we never said out loud.

I'd curl up by the shoes,
knees to my chest,
counting heartbeats
until the house went quiet
and I could pretend
none of it happened.

Sometimes I brought my headphones,
played music I didn't understand
just to drown out
the version of my childhood
they'd never believe.

They thought I was shy.
Quiet.

Well-behaved.
But I was just surviving
one closet at a time.

Now I'm grown.
Moved out.
Safe, they say.

But every now and then,
a smell—
a musty, worn-in mix of dust and denim—
pulls me back.
And I remember
how small I felt
in a space meant for coats
and forgotten shoes.

That closet still holds
the part of me
that never came out.

Shame Sleeps Next to Me

It crawls into bed
when the lights go out.
No warning,
no sound—
just weight.
Heavy as memory.
Sharp as names
I never said again.

Shame doesn't shout.
It whispers.
"You let it happen."
"You wanted it."
"You should've known better."
And I believe it,
more than I believe
in healing,
more than I believe
anyone could love me
if they knew.

I've slept with strangers
just to feel clean.
Just to feel wanted.
Just to feel something
besides this
sticky guilt
that clings to my ribs
and smells like sweat
and old regret.

It wraps around me
like a lover.
Kisses my shoulders
with old flashbacks
and breathes in sync
with my racing pulse.

Some mornings,
I wake up
and it's the first thing I feel.
Not sunlight.
Not peace.
Just shame—
naked,
familiar,
still here.

And I don't push it away.
I just pull the blanket tighter
and pretend
it's something soft.

My Secret's Got Teeth

It doesn't sleep.
It paces.
Gnaws at the inside of my ribs
like it's starving
for the truth
I won't speak.

I buried it deep—
beneath the laugh,
beneath the smile,
beneath the **"I'm fine"**
I've mastered
like second nature.

But secrets don't die.
They wait.
Grow claws.
Grow fangs.
Learn how to howl
in the dark
when the world
finally quiets.

I feed it silence.
Old lies.
The name I won't say.
The memory I keep
chained in the back of my throat
because if I let it out,

I might unravel
for good.

It doesn't ask for much.
Just attention.
Just to be known.
Just to be heard
by someone
who won't run.

But I'm not ready.
Not yet.

So I keep it caged,
even as it bites through bone
and breathes hot
against my spine.

My secret's got teeth.
And some nights,
I swear
it's the only thing
keeping me alive.

Part XIV: Unholy Ground

The Pastor's Hands Didn't Belong There

He wore the robe.
Spoke in tongues.
Said God forgives all things—
but I wasn't asking for forgiveness.
I was asking
why his hands
were under my shirt
when we were supposed
to be praying.

His breath smelled like mints
and manipulation.
He said it was love.
Said God chose me
because I was pure.
But he touched me
like purity was something
he could break.

I wanted to scream.
I wanted to run.
But shame moves slow
when it's dressed in scripture
and cloaked in authority.

No one believed me.
Not even my mother.
She said,
**"Don't say such things.
He's a man of God."**

So I learned
to keep quiet.
To bury my disgust
beneath hymns
and hollow amens.

His hands didn't belong there.
Not in that room.
Not on my skin.
Not in my memory
all these years later—
still shaking,
still stained,
still reaching
in the dark
where faith used to live.

Hail Marys and Hidden Bruises

I knelt on bruises
no one saw.
Said my Hail Marys
with a mouth that tasted
like blood and doubt.

The pew creaked under me,
like it knew I didn't belong there.
Like it could hear
what he did
when the candles were out
and the door was locked
and God looked away.

They told me to pray harder.
To confess more.
To clean my soul
like it was dirty
because I made a noise
when I should've been silent.

Every mark on my skin
was covered
by a sweater,
a smile,
a holy lie
wrapped in Sunday best.

I counted rosary beads
like maybe one of them

would forgive me
for surviving
what no one wanted to believe.

The bruises faded.
The faith didn't.
But it changed shape—
something sharper now.
Something that doesn't flinch
when I say
his name.

I don't kneel anymore.
Not because I stopped believing.
But because kneeling
should never feel
like submission
to pain.

He Preached About Hell While Making Mine

He stood behind the pulpit
spitting fire and fear,
talking about sin
like he didn't wear it
under his suit.

Said hell was for liars,
for lust,
for broken girls
who didn't keep their knees together
and their mouths shut.

But I knew hell.
I knew it like a room.
Like the smell of his cologne
and the creak of the floorboards
outside my bedroom door
when the sermon was over
and the mask came off.

He said God would punish me
if I told.
Said no one would believe
a stained girl
over a clean man
in a white collar.

So I swallowed it.
The shame.

The skin.
The truth.

Every Sunday,
he preached with a voice
full of thunder,
while I sat in the back
wearing long sleeves
and a silence
that felt like burning.

They called him righteous.
Said he had the gift.
But all I ever got
was fear dressed in scripture
and hands
that taught me
how to hate
the word "holy."

Sunday Was the Worst Day

Sunday was supposed to be sacred.
But for me,
it was the worst day.

The day I put on a dress
that felt like armor,
painted on a smile
I couldn't wear any other time,
and walked into a building
that smelled like wax
and hypocrisy.

The songs were sweet,
but the eyes were sharp.
Judging.
Watching.
Pretending they didn't see
what they didn't want to know.

The pews dug into my back.
The sermons dug deeper.
Tales of redemption
and wrath
and women who brought ruin
just by being seen.

I sat next to my mother
and felt the heat of her silence—
how she flinched
when I squeezed her hand,

how she looked away
when I cried during prayer.

They told me to honor the Sabbath.
But how do you honor
a day that breaks you?
That clothes your pain in scripture
and calls it growth?

I hated Sundays.
Still do.
Because God never showed up.
But he always did.

And no one ever asked
why I stopped singing.

When God Was the Villain

I used to pray.
Knees bruised,
hands clenched,
eyes shut tight
like maybe the dark behind my lids
was safer than the one
outside my door.

I prayed for peace,
for protection,
for Him to see
what was happening
under His roof
in His house
by one of His men.

But nothing changed.
No lightning.
No angels.
No wrath.

Just silence.
Like God was waiting
to see how much I could take
before I broke
in His name.

So I stopped praying.
Stopped believing
in mercy

or justice
or the voice in the sky
that let it all happen.

They said I turned my back on God.
But what if He turned first?

What if the villain
wasn't the devil,
but the silence
that came wrapped in scripture
and shame?

I still flinch when I hear hymns.
Still hold my breath
near stained glass.

Because once,
God was the villain in my story—
and no one
came to stop Him.

I Found My Soul Outside the Church

It didn't happen in a pew.
Not beneath stained glass,
not with a Bible in my hand
or a sermon in my ear.

I found my soul
outside the church—
in the quiet,
in the dirt,
in the eyes of a stranger
who didn't quote scripture
but saw I was bleeding
and stayed anyway.

No judgment.
No psalms.
Just presence.
And that was holier
than anything I ever heard
echo through a pulpit.

They told me I'd be lost
without God.
But it turns out,
I was only lost
inside their walls—
where forgiveness had a price
and silence
was the tithe they expected me to pay.

Outside,
the sky didn't accuse me.
The wind didn't flinch.
And when I cried,
the earth didn't tell me
to keep it down
for decency's sake.

I still believe in spirit.
But not the kind
that hides behind collars
and crosses.
I found it
in survival,
in truth,
in the fire that kept me warm
long after the church
locked its doors.

Part XV: What Survived the Fire

I'm Still Here, Even If I Limp

I don't walk like I used to.
Not just my stride—
but the way I enter rooms,
the way I trust chairs,
the way I brace
for conversations
that might shatter
if I say the wrong truth.

Some people see strength
in survival.
But they don't see the limp.
The tilt of the spine
from years spent bent
under names I never asked for,
from nights that bruised my sleep
into silence.

I used to hide it—
the slowness,
the scar that won't fade,
the wince when someone hugs too hard.
Now I let them see.
Because healing isn't a clean line.
It's a crawl.
It's a climb.
It's a whisper that says
"Keep going"
even when the road is ash
and your shoes are gone.

I don't walk like I used to.
But I'm still walking.
Still rising.
Still stubborn enough
to take another step
just to prove
I made it
through a fire
that thought it could kill me.

My Scars Make a New Map

I used to trace my scars
like they were mistakes,
like every mark
was proof
I got it wrong.

Now I see a map—
not back to where I came from,
but forward.
Each line a road I survived.
Each burn a turn I took
when no one else was guiding me.

They tell you scars are ugly.
But mine?
They shine in the mirror
like landmarks.
Like I've been places
most people won't admit exist.

There's one across my wrist
that says I stayed.
One down my thigh
that says I left.
One on my back
that says someone tried
to break me
and failed.

No GPS would follow this path.
No clean story
could fit all these turns.
But I'm not looking
for a pretty journey.

I'm just trying
to keep going.

And when I get lost,
I don't ask for directions—
I look at the skin
that never forgot
where I've been.

Soft Things That Didn't Die

They tried to burn the tenderness out of me—
with fists,
with silence,
with nights that taught me
love could come with a price
and a bruise.

But some things refused to die.
Like the way I still cry at movies.
The way I hum
when I wash dishes.
The way I still believe
sunlight through a window
can mean something
if you let it.

I held onto softness
with both hands,
even when it felt like weakness.
Even when they told me
I'd be safer
if I hardened.

But I've seen what hard does.
I've seen how it breaks things
from the inside out.
I've seen people lose themselves
trying not to feel
what made them human.

So I stayed soft.
Even when it hurt.
Even when it made me
a target.
Even when it felt
like a flaw.

And now?
It's my armor.
My proof.
That kindness can live
through fire
and still bloom
in the ash.

Hope Doesn't Have to Be Loud

It doesn't shout.
Doesn't wave flags
or make speeches
or light up the sky
like some miracle.

Most days,
hope is a whisper—
barely there,
barely breathing.
Just enough
to make you get up
when the bed feels like an anchor.

It's in the way
you wash your face
after crying.
The way you answer the phone
even when you don't want to talk.
The way you plant something
just to see if it grows.

Hope isn't loud.
It's the sound
of your own breath
after you thought
you'd stopped wanting to hear it.

It's the quiet "maybe"
when everything else
says no.

I used to think
hope had to look like power.
Now I know
it just has to last
long enough
to get you through
today.

And that's enough.
Even if no one else sees it.
Even if it's just a flicker
you hold
in your chest
when the dark comes back.

Faith on Fire, Soul Still Singing

I set my faith on fire
when it stopped feeling like home.
Watched it burn—
page by page,
prayer by prayer,
until the smoke
smelled like freedom.

They said I'd be lost without it.
Said the flames would consume me.
But sometimes you have to burn
what was built to cage you
just to see
if there's anything left underneath.

And there was.
A soul.
Cracked,
but still whole enough
to hum a tune
that wasn't borrowed
from anyone else's god.

I don't kneel anymore.
But I still speak to the stars.
Still believe in mercy
that isn't bought with guilt.
Still sing—
not hymns,
but the kind of song

your bones remember
when silence feels too loud.

They said I walked away from faith.
But maybe I just carried it
somewhere safer.
Somewhere warm.
Somewhere it could breathe.

Faith burned.
But the soul?
The soul
still sings.

This Time I Didn't Apologize for Living

I used to say sorry
for everything.
For crying too loud.
For needing too much.
For taking up space
in rooms that made me feel
like I wasn't invited.

I apologized
for my survival—
for making it out
when others didn't,
for the rage I carried,
for the way healing
didn't always look polite.

But not this time.

This time,
I stood up
without shrinking.
Breathed deep
without explaining why.
Took the last piece of bread,
the front seat,
the right to speak
without permission.

I didn't justify
the weight of my existence.

Didn't smooth the edges
or soften the truth
just to make someone else
more comfortable.

I lived.
Messy.
Loud.
Unapologetically present.
And if that unsettled anyone—
so be it.

I've bent myself
into silence for too long.
This time,
I didn't apologize
for living.

And I won't
ever again.

Author's Note

This book was never meant to be comfortable.
It was meant to be honest.

The Gospel According to the Broken is not a collection of
polished prayers or tidy lessons. It is a raw testimony—each
poem a witness to the things we're told not to talk about. Abuse.
Addiction. Abandonment. Grief. Poverty. Shame. Survival.
These are the stories we bury under headlines, under judgment,
under silence.

But silence is where pain multiplies.

I wrote this book for the people no one writes for. The ones who
have slept in shelters and churches and jail cells. The ones who
have stood in clinic waiting rooms, whispered their traumas to a
mirror, and survived more than most will ever understand. I
wrote it for the ones who carry their faith in fractured pieces
and find their hope in places far from stained glass and steeples.

These poems were born from truth—some mine, some
borrowed, all real. They come from the dark corners of our
world that are too often ignored by those with power, and too
often walked through alone by those without it.

If you saw yourself in these pages,
you are not alone.
If you didn't,
I hope you listened.

— *Brandon Michaels*